I See a Star

by JEAN MARZOLLO

Illustrations by SUSE MACDONALD

Cartwheel
B·O·O·K·S

SCHOLASTIC INC.

New York   Toronto   London   Auckland   Sydney
Mexico City   New Delhi   Hong Kong   Buenos Aires

For the Barton family,
with memories of wonderful
Christmas pageants
—J.M.

Special thanks to Jenna, who helped make the costumes;
to Aimee, Dee, Annie, Luke, Jamie, Libba, Max, Hunter, Henry,
Nick, Brittany, Kas, Garret, George, Dale, Parker, Ron, Harry,
Mikayla, and Molly, who posed for the illustrations;
and to Jude, Casey, and Jean, who helped me
pull it all together.
—S.M.

ISBN 0-439-26616-5

Text copyright © 2002 by Jean Marzollo.
Illustrations copyright © 2002 by Suse MacDonald.
All rights reserved. Published by Scholastic Inc.
SCHOLASTIC, CARTWHEEL BOOKS, and associated logos are trademarks
and/or registered trademarks of Scholastic Inc.

12 11 10 9 8 7 6 5 4 3 2   02 03 04 05 06

Printed in Singapore   46
First Scholastic printing, October 2002

Rebus Key

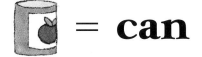 = can

 = you

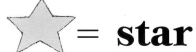 = see

a = a

 = star

 = I

 = camel

 = king

 = shepherd

 = sheep

 = donkey

 = cow

= dove

= angel

= Joseph

= Mary

= Baby Jesus

UCa ?

Ca .

UC3s?

C3s.

🥫 U C 3 🧎 s ?

👁 C 3 🧎 s .

[CAN] U C 2 [SHEEP] ?

[EYE] C 2 [SHEEP].

U C a ?

C a .

UC2s?

C2s.

UC3 s?

C3 s.

UCa?

Ca.

 C

1 ☆

1

3 s

3 s

2

1

2 s

1

3 S

1

1

1

I Can't.

I C 20 ★ s.